Timbo Makes a Splash!

It was an exciting day for Meadowsweet Farm because the new owners, Farmer Morris, his wife and their two children, Edward and Sally, were arriving. All at the farm were looking forward to the arrival of the new owners - but none more than Timbo the old tractor.

Timbo had been retired many years before when a new, more powerful tractor had come to the farm. He had been parked at the back of the barn where, gradually, he had got buried beneath a mountain of old hay until everyone forgot he was there.

Timbo was very sad for he loved to work on the farm. Now only the chickens used him as a perch. Timbo hoped the new Farmer would give him the chance to work again.

The Adventures of Timbo the Tractor

Timbo Makes a Splash!

This book belongs to

_____

_____

_____

_____

Story by Cheryl Foster
Illustration by Armand Foster

Van Molle Publishing

First Published in Great Britain 1995 by
Van Molle Publishing
PO Box 29
Boncath
Dyfed SA43 1YN

First Edition 1995
Second Edition 1996

Printed in Wales by Cambrian Printers, Aberystwyth

ISBN 0-9526925-0-3

The very next morning Farmer Morris walked into the barn with Edward and Sally.

"Now, children," he told them, "the first thing we've got to do is clean up this barn."

"What's that?" Edward asked, seeing Timbo's red roll bar sticking out of the hay.

Farmer Morris looked to where Edward was pointing.

"Well, I'm blowed!" he exclaimed. "It looks as if there might be a tractor under all that hay. Let's find out."

Farmer Morris and Edward each took a spade. It took half an hour of digging but finally Timbo began to emerge. But, oh dear, he did look a very sorry tractor indeed with dirt and hay covering him from his roll bar to his tyres.

Farmer Morris gave Timbo a quick check over.

"Everything seems to be in good order. Let's try the engine."

Very carefully, Farmer Morris poured fuel from a can into Timbo's tank, then turned the ignition key. It was all the encouragement that Timbo needed. He burst into life and the children clapped their hands in delight.

"Now, children, you can get to work cleaning up this old tractor!" Farmer Morris declared before slowly driving Timbo out of the barn and into the warm sunshine.

"What's going on here?" squealed a voice from across the yard. The call came from a large pink pig looking over the sty wall who, with his friends, watched in amusement as the children got busy with buckets of hot water and scrubbing brushes.

"Wow!" exclaimed Edward. "This is really hard work." But soon Timbo's green body and his red roll bar began to sparkle and gleam. Timbo smiled. It felt so good to be clean again.

Pleased with their efforts, Sally and Edward called to their father to come and look.

"Well done, children." said Farmer Morris after inspecting their work. "You've done a good job. But I wonder if either of you have noticed the number plate at the back?"

Sally and Edward both shook their heads. Curious, they walked round to the back of the tractor.

"T.1.M.B.O." Sally slowly spelt out. Then she laughed. "It looks like it says 'Timbo'!"

"That's right," said her father, "and I think Timbo will prove very useful around the farm."

Timbo could hardly believe what he was hearing. He was going to be useful again!

"Now," continued Farmer Morris to the children, "I'm going to check the animals. You can come with me if you like."

They left Timbo in the yard but as they walked through the gate, Timbo noticed that the latch had not been properly closed. He decided he would visit the animals too!

Timbo switched his engine on, nudged the gate open and merrily chugged across the field.

It was not long before he was surrounded by some curious sheep. "Hello!" he announced. "I'm Timbo the Tractor and I shall be bringing you your hay in future."

This pleased the sheep and they wanted him to stay but Timbo was impatient to move on.

"I'm sorry, I can't spend all day talking to you, I must go and see the cows."

Timbo was so busy saying hello to the cows that he did not notice the bull standing behind the bushes, nor the sign by the gate saying 'BEWARE!'.

A sudden cry startled Timbo.

"STOP! STOP! Somebody stop that thief!"

Timbo hurried to the gate and looked across to the next field. It had recently been ploughed and in the centre Mr. Scarecrow stood shouting.

"Stop him! He's got my trousers. I shall catch cold without them!"

Timbo saw the culprit - Godfrey the goat - running across the field, a pair of blue striped pyjamas in his mouth. Timbo did not know what to do.

"I'm sorry," he called to Mr. Scarecrow, "but I can't open the gate and dare not crash through it. Anyway I haven't enough fuel to go chasing goats."

Timbo watched, horrified, as the goat stopped and with a mischievous twinkle in his eye, gobbled up Mr. Scarecrow's trousers!

Timbo quickly decided he had better return to the cows! But no sooner had he started back than he had to screech to a halt - for there blocking his path was a huge brown bull.

"And what's going on here?" the bull bellowed at Timbo. "Who gave you permission to come into *my* field and disturb *my* cows?"

Timbo was so afraid that he did not wait to answer. Instead he reversed as fast as he could - straight into a hedge! He peered out, trembling with fear whilst the bull stood, watching and snorting in disgust.

"Oh dear," groaned Timbo, "I can't get past the bull. Now I shall have to find another way home." He backed his way out of the hedge and looked around. He was surprised to find himself in the ploughed field where Mr. Scarecrow lived. Timbo hoped Mr. Scarecrow was not still cross with him.

Cautiously approaching Mr. Scarecrow, Timbo gave a timid cough before asking whether there was a way back to the farm that avoided the bull.

"Certainly." said Mr. Scarecrow, pointing with his left arm. "You can go that way."

"Thank you ever so much." squeaked a relieved Timbo, surprised that the scarecrow had been so helpful. He hurried across the field. It was getting late and he had to get back before anyone noticed he was missing.

"That was naughty!" laughed the crow perched on Mr. Scarecrow's arm. "You forgot to mention he has to cross the duck pond to get home!"

"Exactly," smiled Mr Scarecrow smugly. "That will teach him not to help me when I ask."

At that moment they heard a terrible wail as Timbo, travelling too fast to stop, flew off the edge of the bank.

"Oh no!" Timbo cried out as he saw the water.

But nothing could save him. His wheels just spun uselessly round and round in the air as he plunged down and down.

"Look out!" the leaping fish warned each other as with an ENORMOUS splash, Timbo landed in the water.

Timbo was horrified to find himself radiator deep in water. He tried to re-start his engine but it only coughed and spluttered before falling completely silent.

"What shall I do now?" Timbo asked the ducks and rabbits who had gathered round to see what had caused all the commotion. But they could not help him. Timbo felt very miserable indeed and blew forlornly on his horn. Fortunately, Farmer Morris and the children heard him as they returned from the fields.

Farmer Morris looked at Timbo in the water. He scratched his head in amazement.

"Well I'm blessed if I know how the tractor got here. We'll have to ask Farmer Smith if he can send Big Red Tractor over to pull him out."

It seemed a very long time to Timbo before he heard the roar of Big Red Tractor's engine coming to his rescue. By now the water had made him very cold.

Big Red Tractor was not at all pleased with Timbo. He considered himself far too important to be dragging old tractors out of ponds.

"I suppose I shall have to pull you out," he told Timbo crossly, "otherwise we shall be here all night. You'd better do what you can to help."

"I'm sorry," sobbed Timbo, "but my engine won't work at all."

"Typical!" huffed Big Red Tractor as he strained to pull Timbo out of the water. At first nothing happened. Timbo's wheels remained stubbornly stuck in the mud.

"Phew!" puffed Big Red Tractor. "This is harder than I thought." He revved his engine, grimacing with the effort, and tried once more.

At last Timbo could feel himself move and slowly he came clear of the water.

"Thank you Big Red Tractor. Thank you!" he spluttered, so pleased to be back on dry land.

"Well," scolded Big Red Tractor, "I hope that has taught you to look before you leap!"

"Oh it has. I've certainly learnt my lesson." Timbo promised.

"Very well then," Big Red Tractor relented, "hold on to the tow rope and I'll pull you back to the farm."

So Big Red Tractor towed Timbo to the farmyard where all the animals, who by now had heard of Timbo's adventure, waited to greet him.

After waving goodbye to Big Red Tractor, Farmer Morris gave Timbo a careful examination.

"No harm seems to have been done." he finally declared. "A day to dry out and he should be as good as new."

"Hooray!" chorused the children. "Then tomorrow we'll give Timbo another polish."

"I still don't understand how Timbo came to be in the water." Farmer Morris was heard to say to the children as they walked back to the house.

The animals knew but kept quiet. Timbo, they decided, had been in enough trouble for one day!

Timbo just smiled. It was so good to be back safe and sound amongst his new found friends.